Harry and His Bucket Full of Dinosaurs

Let's Go to the Moon!

Based on the original stories created by
Ian Whybrow and Adrian Reynolds

PUFFIN BOOKS
Published by the Penguin Group: London, New York,
Australia, Canada, India, Ireland, New Zealand and South Africa
Penguin Books Ltd, Registered Offices: 80 Strand, London WC2R 0RL, England

puffinbooks.com

First published 2008
1 3 5 7 9 10 8 6 4 2

Made and printed in China
ISBN: 978–0–141–50183–3

Harry and his friend Charley were eating their sandwiches and talking about the moon.

"Nan says it's made of cheese, like my sandwich," said Harry.

Charley disagreed. "No, it's made of chunky peanut butter, like mine."

"Let's ask Sid," said Harry. "He's very clever!"

Sid was sure that the moon was made of rocks and pebbles.

"Has anyone ever thought that maybe the moon is made of cookies?" Trike added.

"I know! We'll just go to the moon and find out!" said Harry.

"We can't go to the moon!" said Charley. "It's too far away, and we would need a big rocket to get there."

"Not from here maybe," said Harry, "but I bet we could get there from Dino World!"

"One, two, three . . . JUMP!" the dinosaurs shouted, as Harry and Charley bounced on the bed and then disappeared into the bucket.

When they landed in
Dino World, there it was . . .

the
biggest,
shiniest
moon rocket
they had ever seen!

"Let's go!" said Harry.
But first Sid had to get
something . . .

He came back with a huge backpack strapped to his back.

"What's that for, Sid?" asked Harry.

"It's food," Sid replied. "We'll need a picnic if the moon is made of dust and pebbles as I suspect."

"No we won't," said Harry. "The moon is made of cheese."

"Peanut butter!" Charley shouted.

"Cookies!" Trike joined in.

"Better safe than sorry," said Sid.
They all squeezed into the rocket and the countdown began.

FIVE . . .

FOUR . . .

THREE . . .

TWO . . .

ONE . . .

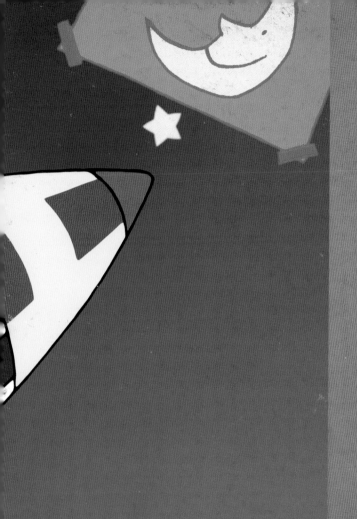

WE HAVE LIFT OFF!

"To the moon!" they all shouted delightedly as the rocket blasted off.

Harry and Taury watched Dino World getting smaller as they zoomed towards the moon.

When they landed, they all bounced and somersaulted out of the rocket. With no gravity on the moon, even the dinosaurs were weightless.

"Wheeeee! This is fun!"

they all cried.

"It's time to find out what the moon is really made of," said Harry. He got out his magnifying glass and looked closely. "I hate to say it," he said, "but it looks as if Trike was right!"

"Mmm, delicious!" said Charley, popping a chunk of moon into her mouth. "Chocolate-chip cookie!"

"I told you so! I told you so!" said Trike, jumping around triumphantly.

"Don't you just hate it when Trike is right!" said Taury. But no one could remember it ever happening before.

"How did all these big holes get here?" Charley wondered.
Harry looked at the dinosaurs tucking into the yummy
moon and then he realized . . . someone had been eating
the moon!

ROAR-R-R-R!

Suddenly a loud roar made the moon shake.
"What was that?" said Charley trembling.
"It sounds like a big . . . scary . . . moon-eating monster,"
replied Harry. "And it's coming this way!"

"It looks more silly than scary," said Charley from behind a big rock, as the monster came into view.

The monster sniffed the air and began running towards their hiding place. Harry, Charley and the dinosaurs ran away, but the monster only seemed to be interested in Sid.

Sid ran as fast as he could, but his heavy backpack weighed him down. Luckily the backpack fell off and the monster suddenly stopped.

"Look, everyone," said Harry. "He wasn't
trying to catch us. All he wanted was Sid's picnic."
Harry bravely walked up to the monster.
"Scrummy-umptious!" said the monster, licking his lips. "I haven't
tasted anything this good in ages!"

The monster explained that since his spaceship had crashed on the moon, he had eaten nothing but chocolate-chip cookie – and now he really wanted a change!

Then the monster became sad. He thought that when Harry and the dinosaurs left, he'd be alone again, with no other food to eat.

Harry had an idea.

"Why don't you take our rocket back home," he said.
All the monster had to do was take them back to
Dino World first.

When they landed in Dino World, Harry, Charley and the dinosaurs all said goodbye to the monster.

"Maybe we could visit your planet one day," said Charley, "we could bring another picnic."

"One small request . . ." replied the monster.

"We know," they all laughed.

"No chocolate-chip cookies!"

When they got back home, Nan came in
with more sandwiches.
"Mmm, banana!" said Harry. He was delighted
they weren't cheese again. Nan always
made him cheese sandwiches.
Harry thought of the moon monster.
It WAS good to have a change!